The Pumpkin Patch

story and photographs by Elizabeth King

Dutton Children's Books   New York

I am grateful to Joe and Janet Cicero, Cicero Farms;
to my husband, Dale Ettema; and to my editor, Lucia Monfried.
Special thanks to Faulkner Farms; Candy Jaeger; Teri Koenig;
Cindy Lieberman; Tim McKibben; Kathleen Minor; Laura Numeroff;
Tapia Bros. Inc.; Stephen Trimble; Bud Vom Cleff; Valley Sod
Farms; and last, and most importantly, the farm laborers of
the San Fernando Valley.

Library of Congress Cataloging-in-Publication Data

King, Elizabeth, date
  The pumpkin patch/story and photographs by Elizabeth King.—
1st ed.
     p.   cm.
  Summary: Text and photographs describe the activities in a
pumpkin patch, as pink-colored seeds become fat pumpkins,
ready to be carved into jack-o'-lanterns.
  ISBN 0-525-44640-0
  1. Pumpkin—Juvenile literature. [1. Pumpkin.] I. Title.
SB347.K56   1990
635'.62—dc20   89-25938 CIP AC

Published in the United States by
Dutton Children's Books,
a division of Penguin Books USA Inc.

Designer: Alice Lee Groton

Printed in Hong Kong
First Edition   10 9 8 7 6 5 4 3 2 1

For my father, James C. King,
who led the way
with a silver sunbeam.

It's autumn. The days are cool and crisp. The wind rustles the cornstalks and shakes the leaves from the trees. Down the dusty road in the pumpkin patch, the pumpkins are round and ripe. They are ready to be picked.

This pumpkin patch is part of a large vegetable farm. The farmer grows peppers, corn, and squash. Pumpkins are a type of squash.

A lot of work was done in the pumpkin patch before the pumpkins were ready to be picked and carved into Halloween jack-o'-lanterns.

Work begins in July. The farmer prepares the soil in his fields for the pumpkin seeds.

First, a plow slices and turns over the earth.

Next, the ground is smoothed by a machine. Then straight rows are marked in the fields.

A crew of workers plants the pumpkin seeds in the rows. With a hoe, a man digs a hole in the ground. Another man drops a couple of seeds in the hole and then covers the seeds with earth.

Pumpkin seeds come from inside pumpkins. The seeds are creamy white in color. But the seeds the farmer buys from the seed company have been coated with a pink powder. This chemical keeps the seeds from being eaten by underground insects after the seeds are planted.

Under the warm earth, the seeds begin to sprout. After a week, two leaves appear where each seed was planted. These first leaves are called seed leaves.

Next, pumpkin vine leaves appear. These leaves are a different shape. They have jagged edges and feel prickly. The leaves grow quickly.

The pumpkin plants have been placed far enough apart to leave room for the pumpkin vines to spread. Before the plants get too big, the farmer weeds between the rows. Weeds take away water and food from the growing pumpkin plants.

More new leaves grow. Stems grow too. The stems twist and crawl along the ground as they become vines.

Curly tendrils appear on the vines. They wrap themselves around other parts of the plants to help the vines spread.

The vines become thick and strong. Soon they will be long enough to touch one another between the rows.

The leaves look like big hands covering the earth.

Meanwhile, flowers begin to bloom on the vines.

Some of the pumpkin flowers sit on top of little green bulbs. These little bulbs will swell beneath the flowers.

They are baby pumpkins!

With water and sunlight, the little green pumpkins grow bigger and bigger. The pumpkins are hard to find among the leaves because they are the same color. But they do not stay hidden for long.

The pumpkin skins slowly turn from green to orange.

By the middle of October, the pumpkins are plump and orange all over. They are ready to be picked.

First, the workers cut the vines to untangle them. Then they cut the stems of the pumpkins with big shears.

The farmer's family decorates the farm stand
for Halloween. They place pumpkins all around
on the soft straw. They hope customers will
want to stop at the stand with the wicked witch,

the scarecrow,

and the papier-mâché pumpkin that is big enough to walk into.

There are piles and piles of pumpkins that have been grown on the farm. They come in different sizes and different shapes.

Some have smooth skins.

Others have big bumps.

Some are big,

and some are little.

Children come to the patch to pick out their pumpkins.

They see and touch the pumpkins. They roll them on the ground and hold them up. This squash makes a great crown.

This pumpkin is round and smooth, with a good strong stem for the lid of a jack-o'-lantern.

When he sells his pumpkins, the farmer's work is done for the year. Now it's time for the children to take their pumpkins home and carve them.

With a candle inside, the pumpkin glows on Halloween night.
Ghosts and goblins, BEWARE!